Looking for the Fire

a Firehawks romance story

by

M. L. Buchman

Other works by M.L. Buchman

The Night Stalkers
The Night Is Mine
I Own the Dawn
Daniel's Christmas
Wait Until Dark
Frank's Independence Day
Peter's Christmas
Take Over at Midnight
Light Up the Night

Firehawks
Pure Heat
Wildfire at Dawn
Full Blaze

Angelo's Hearth
Where Dreams are Born
Where Dreams Reside
Maria's Christmas Table
Where Dreams Unfold
Where Dreams Are Written

Dieties Anonymous
Cookbook from Hell: Reheated
Saviors 101

Thrillers
Swap Out!

One Chef!

SF/F Titles
Nara
Monk's Maze

Buchman Bookworks

Looking for the Fire

1

Tess Weaver had been waiting for this moment for months. Like a racehorse out of the gate she'd counted down; seasons, weeks, days, hours…

She hadn't slept a wink last night, caught in some half-waking nightmare that the freedom that beckoned from so close by would be torn away.

But the morning shone bright with that crystalline blue that could only exist above the Lolo National Forest which thrived along the Idaho-Montana border.

The snows had released their stranglehold on the Selway-Bitterroot wilderness and the trails were finally open to her favorite season of the year, fire season.

Always sounded crazy that way, but since it was only inside her head, it didn't really matter. Did it?

Tess left behind the main roads, then the paved ones. Soon she was winding her little pickup along a narrow forest road. The only tracks were the team that had come up to inspect for washouts and clear downed trees. Now it was just her.

She was done with the seven grinding months of working Missoula bars. Six beers, four shooters. Another round of eight Jell-O shots and a pitcher of something dark—that table wouldn't know the difference anymore if she shit in the pitcher rather than filling it with the most expensive stout on tap. (Sometimes her sense of humor was the only thing that survived those nights.) Five orders of, *Hell no, I'm not going home with you.* Two scotch rocks neat.

And if you call me "Hey, Blondie!" once more you'll be wearing this pitcher rather than drinking it. Three more pints of lager, one of pale ale, and a whiskey sour. Two more servings of *Hell no...*

Her looks earned the attention, and more importantly the big tips, but that didn't mean she was going to choose herself a man that even thought of coming near a place like that.

No idea where else she was going to find "him," but it wasn't at the Spotted Pony Bar.

For seven months she'd done her servitude in the kick-ass cowboy bar in Missoula filled with broke college students and rich skiers come to conquer Montana Snowbowl by skiing all thirty-nine trails without dying in the process. Half of the runs were "Black Diamond"—most difficult—trails; that should kill at least of some of these dweebs, shouldn't it? Few made it more than a dozen runs before getting trapped in the swirl of this bar and a dozen more just like it that lined the road from the mountain into town—a strip locals avoided like the plague around two a.m. last call. Even the cops were careful driving this stretch after midnight.

Tess was finally done with bowing to the holy paycheck and getting home at three a.m. after clearing out and cleaning up the place before she could finally take off her mandatory cowgirl hat—at least the damn thing didn't have to be pink though a lot of the waitresses went that way at the Spotted Pony. The last time an Appaloosa had been near the place was probably during the 1877 retreat of the Nez Perce peoples; it was just that authentic.

Tess parked Snow Cone, her battered white Toyota pickup truck that no longer had a third gear, but thankfully second and fourth were still going strong, at the very end of the fireroad and took a breath.

Then another.

The city did that to her, even a small city like Missoula.

Made her way cynical right when she least expected it.

She was always torn that way. The social whirl could be fun and it was nice to be able to get a decent burger or a slice of pizza when you wanted to. Catching an action flick on the big screen had its points as well.

But it was the shorter half of the year that she lived for.

For the next five months she'd be queen of one of the most least accessible fire lookout towers anywhere in the Idaho wilderness. Far enough out that the only visitors were either crazy, or crazier.

She climbed out and leaned back against her truck, closing her eyes and just letting the thick forest air wash the city off her.

The merely crazy people who'd reach her tower atop Cougar Peak—eight miles from the nearest road and 8,859 feet into the sky—were very like her; out to walk, fish, and camp in one of the toughest and wildest forests left in the lower forty-eight states. The Bitterroots might top out around nine and ten thousand where the Beartooths to the east and the Lemhis to the west in Idaho cracked twelve, but for expanse and ruggedness and sheer cussed toughness of country, she'd vote for the Bitterroots any day. So, the merely crazy folks might stop for a day if they reached her lookout.

The crazier people would whip through in an hour. They were the ones walking the CDT. The Continental Divide Trail was way high and seriously tough. The south-bounders still had a month before the snow in Glacier Park backed off enough to begin their trek from Canada to Mexico.

The northbound walkers wouldn't reach her until later in the fire season because they'd begun back in March or April down where Mexico shared her border with New Mexico, a hundred miles into the harsh desert south of the Gila National Forest. By the time they'd spent six months afoot, they'd be racing the snows to the Canadian border. They blew through the Lolo so fast that she sometimes didn't even have a chance to come down from her lookout tower to greet them before they were gone again from her small meadow.

That meant, for five months, the vast quiet would be hers. She couldn't wait.

Two weeks up, three days down in town or off camping in the wild while a substitute came in. Repeat until the end of the fire season chased her back down, at times barely steps ahead of the first heavy snow. Over the last five seasons she'd ridden out plenty of early blizzards while still monitoring fires as they chewed through the valleys that spread thousands of feet below her. Only once had she been caught by a true snow and that had been seriously bad; a mistake she wouldn't make again.

Tess shouldered her pack and took a deep breath. The tang of hot engine metal from the slow climb up the forest road that was little more than a dozer track. And...

There it was.

Nothing like it down in the valleys. High forest, bright with pine and sunshine but still thick with fern, berry, and sumac undergrowth. You could practically smell the wildlife watching her from the trees, assessing this new intruder.

Not new, she reassured them. *Same chick as last year and the one before. Back to watch the fire.*

The distinct "pik" call and hard rattle of a downy woodpecker somewhere back in the trees released the other birds and the woods came back to a symphony of life that had been momentarily frozen by the wheezing arrival of her truck.

Her pack weighed fifty pounds and would be grueling by the time of her noon when she'd hiked the last five thousand feet and seven miles up to her lookout. She really shouldn't have bagged out on her winter workouts so often. She'd be hurting by the time she arrived.

Didn't matter, she was headed into the hills.

Another three hundred pounds of supplies remained heaped in the truck bed under a tarp. In a couple days a mule team, who made much of its spring income ferrying stock up to the lookouts, would come by and do the heavy lifting for her.

Tess patted her truck on the hood where it would sit and wait for ten days and turned toward the perfect solitude of the trees.

2

Jack Parker waved as Burt drove off. An arm raised casually out the window, a downshift to ease around the first curve, and his buddy was gone.

Jack stood by the trailhead. They'd unloaded a huge mound of supplies at the head of the road, which thankfully wasn't his task to buck up to the lookout. He pulled on his pack and faced the great unknown. Fir trees towered above him so tall they looked ready to topple down and kill him where he stood.

Stoopid!

Clarie and Mitch always made their summers up here sound so friggin' romantic. So, when Clarie found out she was pregnant and would be delivering right in the middle of the summer, he hadn't put up too much of a fuss about taking their place for a season. Not as if he had anything better to do.

He was used to living a little rough.

Retired Army, four years in the dustbowl. All of it living in CHUs with a couple hundred other grunts assigned to the Containerized Housing Units—which was just as luxurious as it sounded. Living rough wouldn't be an issue.

And landing in Montana due to lack of any other prospects was eating at his ego and his body. Burt, his college roommate, had given him the couch space cheap. But after two months it had given him a permanent kink in the back and he still didn't know what to do with himself.

So, he was going to sit by himself, stare at empty wilderness for hours waiting for a puff of smoke, and get his head screwed back on straight.

Yeah, that made perfect sense. Not.

Clarie said the trailhead was easy to find. After fifteen minutes of floundering through blackberry thorns and checking his cell phone a half dozen more times for signal strength that it didn't have the first time, he finally stumbled on it. It *was* easy to find, once you found it. Standing a few feet apart, two knee-high boulders marked what might be the entry into Mirkwood— an evil forest grown even more dire since the hobbits voyage on the way to slay the fire-breathing dragon.

Fire.

He was headed to the top of a mountain to face a forest that breathed fire.

"Okay, Mirkwood. Here we go."

He resettled his pack with a grunt; he hadn't done a long hike with a full ruck since Basic. He'd been driving a MaxxPro MRAP for the last four years, and better yet, lived to tell about it. Wished he could have brought his fifteen-ton Mine Resistant Ambush Protected beast home. Blown up seven times and only lost two guys total out of a half jillion trips with ten troops typically onboard for each ride. An IED had blown out half their tires, then been followed up by a couple of T-men lying in wait for them to dismount. Two Army and two Taliban was the body count for that day—only deaths in the whole theater.

Still, it had gotten pretty shaky there toward the end. As the troops drew down, those remaining were blown up more often. Three of the IED strikes had been in his last three weeks in. And the T-man, with fewer targets, was shooting a lot more lead at his MRAP's armor hoping to find a hole. When he lay down to sleep at night, he could still here the deafening rattle of the gunfire pinging off his vehicle.

Not there anymore. Now here. He'd been saying that to himself a lot lately.

The pack. The trail. Hold the focus. Get your heavy-ass load moving.

Of course now, without the "Three A's" of ammo, armor, and more ammo—which still felt weird as hell, like he was walking around naked—the weight he carried wasn't all that different.

He'd grown up in downtown Phoenix. Going to college in Missoula hadn't exactly turned him into an outdoorsman, neither had driving an MRAP. Most of his time in the wilderness had been during Basic in the swamps and hills of South Carolina.

He inspected the forest as he began the long climb through it. Fir trees, maples, and ferns; those he knew. And blackberry thorns; his arms still itched from all the scratches. The white bark was either birch or aspen. After that, there were bushes and there were trees—his two primary classifications of stuff that grew outdoors. Flowers didn't really count as they mostly grew in expensive florist shops and in girlfriend's vases, while they lasted. There'd been plenty of girls who hadn't lasted as long as the colored blooms.

What had he been thinking? Jack Parker. Wilderness.

Well, at least this trail was clearly marked. He checked his GPS, which suggested a shortcut that Claire had warned him against.

"Your machine doesn't know about the landslide that wiped out that trail three years ago. We had to cut in a new path that summer."

He stuck with the double-white trail blazes Mitch had sprayed on the trees every hundred yards or so.

3

Tess kept her eyes on the trail, not looking at the view. Not yet. Saving that.

Cougar Peak tower was a two-story ten-by-ten foot building perched atop a broad pinnacle of rock.

The only approach was across a small meadow. Beyond that, she hiked the last hundred feet along the guide chain up the bare rock to the mountain's peak.

She entered the lower cabin first.

The cabin only had a normal winter's worth of bug corpses to sweep out; no mice or squirrel had gotten inside to nest this last winter, thank god. They could really mess a place up, leaving stinking patches where the mice peed in their own nests. That took a lot of bleach to clear away.

The water cistern was full to overflowing with rainwater and snowmelt off the tower roof. Best water in the world—tasted of cold sunshine. She dumped out the last of her city water, good riddance, and refilled her bottle from the cistern.

She could feel she was still moving at city pace as she unloaded most of her pack into the rough shelves that were her cupboard. Whatever internal switch that eventually shifted to "move slower" hadn't yet been thrown.

With the cabin squared away and airing out through the open door and four small windows, Tess went back outside and climbed the exterior ladder. It led up to the narrow walkway that encircled the tower's upper story.

She circled the tiny deck that surrounded the tower on all sides, lifting clear the heavy shutters, feeling the sun's warmth radiating off their rough surface. They had protected the big, wrap-around glass windows through the brutal winter storms, but now, for five months, those windows were for her to see the world.

Duck inside—definitely needed to oil the lock—a quick floor sweep and it was all in order.

Out of the small pack she'd brought up from the cabin, she unloaded the last of it. Her radio, spare batteries, solar charger set to one side. Binoculars and the refilled water bottle to the other. Ammonia in a spray bottle and a squeegee. She took her time removing a season's worth of wind-borne mud and dust off the glass.

Then she stood in the center of the tower, the center of her world, and braced her hands on either side of the Osborne Fire Finder.

And let herself look up.

The world slapped her, just as it always did. In some directions she could only see a dozen miles before a ridge or peak blocked her view. In other directions a hundred miles of National Forest sprawled over knife-edge ridges and slashed canyons.

Ten miles to the east lay State Route 12, thankfully invisible at the bottom of a valley. Past that, her view continued in an uninterrupted vista eighty miles to Flathead Lake and the Flathead National Forest beyond.

In all of the 360 degrees, even with her binoculars, the only human habitations she could actually see were two distant cabins and three even more distant lookout towers.

Once her survey was complete, by naked eye and binocular, she grabbed her radio and dialed in the Forest Service frequency.

"Dispatch. Over."

"Dispatch here. Go ahead. Over."

"Cougar Peak in service."

You always reported by your location. Tess liked that. As if she herself embodied the mountain and she could leave her own name mostly behind for the rest of the summer.

"Roger that, Cougar Peak. Glad to have you back, Tess."

"Thanks, Vic. Glad to be here." Vic was the base commander for the whole area.

Tess kicked the single mattress on the narrow bunk, causing it to unroll. She usually slept in the tower, only her supplies below.

She collapsed on it face down. Though the official start of fire season was still over a week away, her internal alarm snapped her awake after only an hour's rest to scan the trees for a telltale puff of smoke that indicated a new fire.

4

"Uh, hello? Testing?"

Tess glared at the radio and wondered what idiot was on the freaking Forest Circus frequency. And more amusingly, just what Vic was going to do to them. This early in the season he was probably going to play nice.

"This is dispatch," Vic always gave someone the benefit of the doubt. That's why he was Dispatch and Tess was locked away in her steel gray-and-wood tower all summer.

She wouldn't trade places for the world.

"This is Jack, uh, I mean Gray Wolf Summit."

"In service," Dispatch prompted.

"Yeah, right. In service."

"Roger that, welcome aboard, Jack."

Wait!

Gray Wolf Summit?

Not stopping to think, she grabbed up her radio, "Who the hell is this?"

Vic knew better than to answer.

"You. Gray Wolf. Who is this?"

"This is Gray Wolf Summit, go ahead."

"Where's Clarie and Mitch?"

"She's having a baby. I'm Gray Wolf for the summer."

Shit! Tess didn't like it. For the next five months her world was made up of the five closest lookout towers—two of which she couldn't see from here but had important overlapping sightlines for pinpointing a blaze. Beyond that there was only Dispatch and the occasional firefighting crew.

And all that was just the way she liked it.

Now, with no one asking her, no warning at all, this new guy. It was like coming home on college break only to find out that your best friend had moved away from next door to Texas or some such ridiculous place.

"Uh, welcome." She did her best not to sound too upset but expected that she didn't really pull it off.

"Is this Tess Weaver?" the radio voice asked. It sounded amused with itself.

"Cougar Peak to you." That didn't come out sounding as funny as she intended.

Laughter came back over the radio. A guy who laughed at her joke rather than assuming she was just plain nasty. Another chunk of city-born bitch shield slid off Tess and tumbled off the tower to shatter on the rocks below.

"Yeah, sorry. This is Tess. You're Jack…" she left it open as a question.

"That's Gray Wolf Summit to you. Over and out."

Well, if that didn't beat all. A guy with a decent sense of humor.

5

Jack left the radio on, though he had no intention of replying.

Not a sputter or a squawk came in.

Clarie had talked about how sweet Tess was; all alone in her tower summer after summer. Mitch's expression had been less forgiving about why she was alone. Princess in a tower or bitch on a rock? He was gonna side with Mitch on this one.

Jack had only one bar on his cell phone off some distant tower. Claire had told him there was reception, but this was sad.

It flickered briefly up to two bars which he found ridiculously encouraging. It made him feel at least somewhat connected. He called Burt to say he'd arrived and wasn't—as his buddy was kind enough to predict at length over their final couple beers last night—ready for immediate evac.

Jack had stayed several beers later than he'd intended; he'd sure enjoyed watching the bartender. Long blondes were generally more trouble than they were worth, but this one had been something special. Not just her figure—which had been decidedly athletic in those tight jeans and cowboy shirt untucked with the tails tied across her flat belly—or her shower of blond hair.

What had really caught him was the combination of an absolutely no-nonsense attitude, yet how easily she laughed and joked with the patrons. It didn't look like a sham, even if it had coaxed an extra ten-spot out of his pocket when Burt left the tip. Lady like that, who looked like that, wasn't gonna be interested in his down-

and-out sorry self anyway. Especially not the night before he left for five months to serve a sentence in solitary.

His lookout tower was an all-in-one cabin in the sky. His toilet was a wooden outhouse fifty feet downslope from his tower. At the top of the tower's thirty-seven steps was a fourteen-foot square box surrounded by glass and topped by a radio antenna and a big-ass lightning rod.

Lightning, hadn't thought about that one.

Or the heavy guy wires that stretched out to every side, bolted into bedrock, to keep what must be titanic winds from wiping his temporary home over the cliff and into the valley that was freakily far below.

He'd had the mandatory couple days of classroom training, but the place was still a goddamn mystery. Mitch had planned to hike in with him to show him the ropes, then he'd sprained his ankle in a game of pick-up ball, so Jack was on his own.

The big two-foot disk of the Osborne Fire Finder stood on a pedestal in the middle of his tower cabin. It had a circular map of the area and a pair of sights mounted on a ring that spun around it.

He studied the map, which covered an enormous area and began picking out landmarks.

East and West Goat Mountains.

Sugarloaf Peak.

Como.

The Lonesome Bachelor.

Yeah, there was a good joke. Corporal Jack Parker (U.S. Army retired) who'd found a job staring at trees. Sure wasn't going to find anyone to cuddle with up here.

Clarie and Mitch were at the dead end of a long, tough trail that only connected to the lookout tower. Last year they'd had three visitors, total. One had been the mule train supplier who'd delivered their stock of goods.

Medicine Point Lookout.

Cougar Peak.

Tess Weaver. He spun the Osborne until it lined up perfectly on the map and then looked through the sights. Once he was sure he knew which peak it was, he grabbed for his binoculars.

His closest neighbor, fifteen miles away. Even the big glasses that Mitch had loaned him barely resolved the lookout tower as separate from the rocks.

Which was just fine.

Didn't need her anyway.

6

Jack was surprised at how quickly the days become routine. He rolled out with first light. Hauled up a gallon or two of water to get him through the day and made a quick breakfast of oatmeal and maple syrup with hot chocolate as the sunrise lit the horizon with a thousand shades of pinks and yellows.

After the sun broke the horizon, he'd go for a quick trail run. Didn't need to go more than five K to work up a good burn. No sweat, it evaporated in the high, thin air, but his muscles and the salt stains on his t-shirt told him he was working it hard on the steep and rugged grades.

Each morning held some surprise. A family of gray squirrels, a doe picking her way ever so delicately through the under-growth, a bear who had surprised the shit out of him.

He'd rounded a sharp bend in the trail, circled around the next boulder, and almost run head on into the bear. His squawk, her furry roar of surprise, and they both instantly headed back the way they'd each come. He'd practically levitated back to the tower, not breaking from a dead sprint for almost a thousand feet of vertical gain. He'd sat and laughed at himself, wondering which of them had been more surprised, but only after he was in his tower and had the trapdoor closed and bolted from the inside.

Then there was the daily radio routine. Nine a.m.

"Bare Cone Lookout in service. No smoke."

"Spot Mountain in service. No smoke."

"Cougar Peak in service. No smoke."

Then it was his turn.

He hadn't spoken directly to Cougar Peak since that first time, but he liked the sound of her voice. Efficient, clear, and well practiced.

Fifteen minutes later he'd stumble through his peak weather report: percent cloud cover, high and low temperatures, relative humidity, wind speed and direction, precipitation, and so on. He was always forgetting one item or another, even though it was listed right there on his log.

Tess Weaver was a machine, rattling it all off in half the time, almost in a single breath, in that totally female voice of hers that was teasing him across the airways. Probably one of those thin desiccated fifty-year olds.

Nine a.m. to six p.m. and they were done. Fires peaked between noon and four when the sun dried out the foliage and the midday heat led to stronger circulating winds. By six, the worst of the day was over.

Except so far there hadn't been anything at all.

Routine broke on the ninth day of his first tenner.

Nine days and there hadn't even been a cloud. He'd run out of guys to text; they were either out of the Army long enough to have busy lives, or they were still soldiers and had even less to say to someone gone civvy.

He'd already read all five books he'd brought, twice. Definitely got to get more during his days off. Maybe some movies, but then he'd need another solar charger, a player, and a bunch of disks because wi-fi on top of the mountain peak, not so much.

"Dispatch, this is Cougar Peak. I have a smoke at three-sixteen point four degrees, approximately fourteen miles. Gray Wolf Summit, can you give me a cross? It might be behind a ridge for you."

Jack felt as if he'd just been electrocuted.

He looked down at the map. Three hundred and sixteen degrees from Cougar Peak. He rested his thumb on the mileage scale. About a thumb width and half for fourteen miles. That put it almost due west of him.

Grabbing his binoculars he hurried to the window. There was an awful lot of country out that way. The next road or town in that direction was Moscow, Idaho a hundred miles away—the great trackless waste of central Idaho.

"I don't see it," he sent after the first couple minutes of searching.

"Try looking closer to you," Cougar's voice came over the radio. She didn't follow that with, "Common beginner's mistake is looking too far away," which he appreciated.

It was…

Holy Crap! The smoke was just one valley over. A thin pillar of white smoke wandering lazily into the air.

"I got it!"

"Okay," Tess teased him. "Take a breath, Big Bad Wolf, and shoot a cross sight so we can triangulate a fix."

He lined up the Osborne, "Two seven three degrees. Dead on."

"Roger that. I make it fourteen point three miles for the cross. Down in the guts of Loco Creek. Your fire."

Jack held his radio with both hands because he needed to hold something to keep his hands steady.

"What do you mean? You spotted it."

"It's in your territory."

His first fire and he got to name it. "How about Harold?"

The laugh that came back over the radio was musical and bright. It shocked the hell out of him. Who knew Cougar Peak could laugh like that. "The name is supposed to relate to the topography. And sorry, my end of Loco burned last year so I already used the obvious name."

"I knew a pretty crazy dude named Harold once." He had a tendency to not bother with body armor and Jack had seen him more than once walk through a hail of bullets unscathed as if he were untouchable. "How about Crazy Creek Fire? You sure that's not just someone's campfire?"

"There's been no lightning, so it actually was someone's campfire. There's only the one smoke, so it's probably not a pyromaniac. Except it's not a campfire anymore. When you can see that much smoke, it's already dug in and burning. Dispatch, we've got the Crazy Creek Fire, credit to Gray Wolf, I'd call it at an acre and growing fast. Just at the end of Forest Road 328-Alpha so watch for a camper or car racing to get off the mountain though they're probably long gone."

"Roger that. We'll get an engine out there to give it a look. Well done. Out."

Jack still felt giddy with adrenaline. He really needed to share it with someone. In the Army there'd always been the other guys in the MRAP that day or the CHU that night. He thought about calling Burt, but he wouldn't really understand.

Something had him picking up the radio.

"Hey, Cougar Peak?"

"Go ahead."

How did you boil such a feeling down into something that could be transmitted through a radio? A feeling as if he'd made a difference. Not just trucked teams back and forth across some section of hell as a living target in a massively armored vehicle, but might actually be saving some forest, even lives.

"Uh, thank you."

Her voice was soft when it came back over the radio, "You're welcome, Mr. Big Bad Gray Wolf. And welcome to the Freaking Forest Circus."

Ha! That was perfect. He was being paid to sit and be bored out of his skull. But in one instant, he'd jumped from useless to really helping. A circus act indeed.

"Roger that, She-lion."

She clicked her transmit button in acknowledgement but didn't speak again.

7

Tess wasn't sure how it had begun.

They'd talked at different times as the number of fires increased with the deepening season. When he spotted his first one on his own, she thought he was going to have kittens. It juiced him up something wild, reminding her of the joy in her first season—a feeling that hadn't diminished with time. It was that was grand to hear someone else who felt that way.

He settled well into working radio relay for the hand crews too deep in the canyons for their bosses to hear. Even on the Colgate Fire—which he'd named for being along Crest Creek—when there were six lines of madness going at once, he handled the radio fine. The airshow on that one had been impressive, huge air tankers lumbering by their towers just a few hundred yards straight out the windows. Helicopters painted black and fire-red whirling through the valleys and ridges. The airborne incident commander circling high above in his plane too busy to keep up with the ground relays. A fine piece of radio work, more than she'd have been able to handle on her first season.

So, the man had both a sense of humor and skills. Probably had a wife and kids down below that he only saw every other weekend. A couple times she came close to asking, but stopped herself. The Forest Service frequency was about business and—

"Hey, Cougar Peak. You there?"

"This is Cougar, go ahead Gray Wolf."

"Wanna dial up four tenths?"

"Sure." After six p.m., they were off the clock unless there was an active blaze close by.

They re-tuned their radios to a frequency off the Forest Service frequency by zero-point-four megahertz. And as the evening waned, they talked about nothing for half an hour before going to sleep with the sun.

On another night he asked, "You play chess?"

"Sure, but I don't have a board up here."

"Bring one after your next break."

And she did. They played radio chess through much of June and the fires of July.

Their three days off every two weeks never matched, so they were connected only eight work days out of every fourteen.

A couple times she almost hiked into Gray Wolf Summit on her days off, but she didn't want to ruin the illusion.

The time in July when her substitute couldn't make it because of car trouble, she gladly skipped the luxury of a city shower and a couple nights at her mom's place in order to stay in the sky and talk to Jack the Big Bad Gray Wolf.

"Tell me about you out in the world."

That stopped her.

"No. No, I don't think so."

"Big secrets?" he teased.

"It's not that." If not, what was it? "I don't want to think about those months. These months are the ones when I'm myself. This is where I belong." Which was true…and a total lame-ass evasion. *I don't want to spoil the illusion.*

She'd had plenty of relationships, with the usual good-bad ratio. Nothing that stuck. Nothing that felt as real as when she sat in the sky and looked down on the world made of forest.

"What do you look like, up there in your Cougar Tower? I need something to go on."

"Sixty-five, round as a washtub, with bottle-red hair, and those stretchy pants in bright paisley green? You?"

"I's jes a bow-legged old cowhand, Ms. She-lion. Thas all I be."

"Your cowboy accent sucks." But still it made her laughter echo about the tower.

"What? Did I sound human there for a moment?"

"No, it wasn't that bad."

During the day, they were all business on the Forest Service frequency. But at night she sometimes fell asleep listening to him talk about his day, not that it was all that different from hers, but she liked to hear about it anyway. He didn't push again about the outside world as July rolled into August.

It was the crash that woke her with a shout of surprise. She'd slept down in the lower cabin that night, though she wasn't sure why.

A moment later, a blinding light filled the cabin brighter than daylight. An instant later, another flash. In the same instant, a deafening of superheated air as it was torn apart shook the walls hard.

There was no point counting seconds, the flash and boom of lightning and thunder were wrapped around each other like crazed lovers gone wild in the dark of the night. Instead she counted strikes, losing track around forty-seven. The tower and the peak were struck as if by a hailstorm of billion-volt hammers of Thor.

When it tapered off, she edged up to a window. The cool night air slipping over the windowsill reeked of ozone.

She'd ridden out some bad storms, though nothing like this. She remembered the terror of the first time a strike had hit her tower while she was in it. And that had been a single strike; this was a seriously wild.

It was rolling north, straight for Gray Wolf Summit. He didn't have a ground-level lower cabin like hers, his tower was his cabin. Jack was going to be right in the thick of it in a minute.

"Jack!" she shouted over her radio. "Jack! Wake the hell up!"

"Huh, what?"

"There's a lightning storm heading your way. Bad one! Do not try to leave your tower. The lightning rod and guy wires are your best protection. Lie on the wooden floor. Get off your bunk and don't touch anything metal. You got that?"

"Got it. I'm under the Osborne table and—" There was an unholy crash over the radio at the same moment she saw the strike from across the fifteen miles.

His scream was one of the most horrific sounds she'd ever heard.

Not surprise. Not fear. Stark terror.

She cried out his name, but there was no answer.

It would be impossible for him to hear under the storm of multiple strikes piling up on him.

No sound but that one scream and the crash of thunder. Fifteen seconds later, the muted roll that was only now starting to reach her through the fifteen miles of ozone-laden air that separated them.

Somewhere in the middle of it he transmitted a garbled message degraded into unintelligibility by the thunder on his end. It sounded like barely controlled panic. He might have shouted for her to keep talking. Actually, it hadn't sounded so controlled.

So she did. Shouting messages of comfort for fifteen seconds, listening for five. Shouting again.

Her voice grew hoarse, but she didn't stop.

Not even to wipe at the tears streaming down her cheeks.

8

Jack heard a voice somewhere. Far away. Calling him back.

Starting and stopping.

Calling to him until he came to.

He'd gone fetal on the floor of his lookout cabin. Cradled to his chest was a radio—it kept calling to him.

A woman.

Cougar Peak.

He managed to double-click the transmit key during her next break.

"Oh thank god!"

He waited for her next words like a drowning man waiting for air.

"I thought you'd been incinerated or something." Her voice was thick, hoarse… as if she'd been shouting for a long time.

"How long?" his voice sounded even worse. The mere whisper hurt like hell.

"Storm moved out twenty minutes ago."

He swallowed and tasted blood. A little testing. Ow, shit! He'd bit his tongue really badly. Bit, hell. Felt like he'd round it for the whole twenty minutes with his molars.

The bitter adrenal taste mixed with the iron of the blood almost made him sick. The only way he managed to resist it was knowing that if he puked all over the cabin floor, he was the one who'd have to clean it up. And god, she'd hear it.

Twenty minutes.

It had felt like twenty hours. He had been trapped in IEDs. Not one or two, but thousands: his MRAP tumbling across a field of them, each roll tossing more dead bodies, more deadly shards of steel, striking more IEDs which made him roll again, and more—

"Talk to me, Tess. It's bad. Just keep talking to me."

So she did. She told him about her first trip into the woods. Her mother taking her to see a lookout tower when she was just six.

"Mom wanted to be a lookout so badly. Did ground-school training and everything. Then the head ranger in charge of assignments said he wasn't going to let a single woman go out into the woods alone—couples and males only. She'd tried a dozen different regions, but they all said the same. It was that same summer she was raped in a city, because cities are so much safer than the deep woods, you know. That's how she had me. She never married."

"Is that why you're out here, She-lion?" He sat up. Every one of his muscles complained. He'd only had PTSD attacks a couple times. Figured it was going away. Yeah, until he rode through the heart of the lightning storm from hell.

"Maybe. First year it probably was. But we hiked in the woods a lot together. She liked, likes to fish. Has a bum knee now, so she can't get up here to see me, but we still walk into fishing spots. I fell in love with the wild on my own. Sometimes it feels like I can't breathe until I'm up here."

God but he could picture her, the goddess of the peaks. The she-lion standing guard over her wilderness.

"How about you?"

"Me?"

"You, Gray Wolf. Why are you out here?"

Why was he?

Truth?

"I couldn't think of anything better to do with my summer."

9

Tess took his phone number at the end of the season, she didn't have a number to give other than her mom's and Tess never gave that out.

"I'll buy the first beer," he'd offered.

She'd been down a week and still hadn't call to take him up on the offer.

Knew the number by heart, had it memorized before she'd lowered and latched the shutters, locked the site down for winter, and hiked down off her mountain with the first snows close behind.

Had almost dialed it from her mom's, but didn't know what to say. After the lightning storm, they'd gone deep. They'd told each other the important stuff, back and forth each night on their private frequency.

She felt as if her every truth had been exposed for him to see. Hollowed out trees, cracked wide to reveal their burned out hearts.

If she spoke to Jack Gray Wolf with no last name…if she met him, would she be able to still be herself? No one else knew what he now knew about her. She'd blow it for sure.

Harry took her back on at the Spotted Pony; bars were a pretty good fit for flaky seasonal work. Good bartenders were little better than itinerant workers, so there was always an opening.

Two lagers. Three tequilas with salt and lime. A pair of boilermakers. Two *Thanks but no thanks*. (That would turn into the *Hell no!* version somewhere in the next seven months as it always did.)

Two guys came and sat at the end of the bar, not with the ease of regulars, but they knew the place.

She kind of remembered them from her last night before the fire season. Not that either had been that memorable. But they'd stayed late on her last night and tipped really well.

Her bartender's eye drifted over one of them, still unmemorable, but stopped on the other.

Was it really the same person? There was a set to the eyes, a depth and certainty that couldn't have been there before.

Someone terribly alive lived in that face and it fit him really well.

Harry served them, but she made a point of using the taps down that end of the bar for the next beers she had to draw.

The night was still quiet enough to overhear their conversation.

"You sure she even exists? Sounds like the horseshit craziest story you ever laid on me."

"She exists. She's real. Way more than you, asshole."

Tess was paralyzed with shock. The beer ran out of the glass over her fingers and began running along her forearm to dribble off her elbow. She startled and slapped the tap closed, wiped her hand and arm with a bar rag.

She'd know that voice anywhere. All summer it had been burned into the landscape of her thoughts until she knew it as well as her own. She knew the shape of every scar on his soul just as he knew the scars on hers.

Tess delivered the beer back down the bar.

Before she could talk herself out of it, she grabbed a pen and a bar napkin and wrote a quick note.

Drawing a fresh pint of the porter he was having, Tess set the napkin down with the message showing and then placed the beer right on top of it without saying a word.

He'd know her voice as surely as she knew his.

Tess turned to the next patron calling for a refill even as he called out a confused, "Who's this from?"

From the corner of her eye, she saw him lift the beer and read the note.

Apply liberally in case of forest fire or light-ning storm. She'd drawn a cougar's paw print for a signature.

He looked at her in absolute shock. She set down the beer she was pouring and turned to face him.

A hundred emotions ran across his features, ones that she found she could read as easily as her own; she might not know the handsome face, but she knew the man behind it so well that she didn't need to. There was no one she knew better, or who knew her better.

With a shout of pure joy, the same shout she heard in her heart each time she entered the wilderness, he vaulted the bar and rushed to stop a single step from her.

"She-lion?" his voice hesitated just as it did on that first fire call, right before he'd whispered that "Thank you" that had melted her heart.

"Hey there, Gray Wolf."

He reached for her, thought better of it, then brushed a finger as lightly down her cheek as the last breeze of a storm clearing off the horizon.

"You're real," he was as breathless as he'd been spotting his first fire.

"Last I checked."

This time when he went to reach for her, she stopped him with a hand against the center of his chest. The shock was as super-charged as a lightning strike and heated her insides to full burn.

"One question."

"Anything."

"What's your last name? Jack, Big Bad Gray Wolf, what?"

"Parker. Jack Parker."

She slid the hand up his chest, cupped his neck with her hand and pulled him down into a kiss. He didn't hesitate a second.

As she melted against him to the cheers of the bar crowd, she had just the least little glimpse of the future, like the first smoke puff that showed early to tell of the fire that would rage through the forest.

No longer the lone princess in her tower. Next year she'd be sharing lookout duties on Cougar Peak, and the year after, and the one after that, and...

About the Author

M. L. Buchman has over 25 novels in print. His military romantic suspense books have been named Barnes & Noble and NPR "Top 5 of the year" and *Booklist* "Top 10 of the Year." In addition to romance, he also writes thrillers, fantasy, and science fiction. In among his career as a corporate project manager he has: rebuilt and single-handed a fifty-foot sailboat, both flown and jumped out of airplanes, designed and built two houses, and bicycled solo around the world. He is now making his living full-time as a writer, living on the Oregon Coast with his beloved wife. He is constantly amazed at what you can do with a degree in Geophysics. You may keep up with his writing at www.mlbuchman.com.

Pure Heat
a Firehawks romance

Steve "Merks" Mercer hammered down the last half mile into the Goonies' Hoodie One camp. The Oregon-based Mount Hood Aviation always named its operation bases that way. Hood River, Oregon—hell and gone from everything except a whole lot of wildfires.

Foo Fighters roared out of the speakers, a piece from his niece's latest mix to try and get him out of his standard eighties "too retro" rock and roll. With the convertible top open, his hair whipped in the wind a bit. Hell today it could be pouring rain until his hair was even darker than its normal black and he wouldn't care. It felt so damn good to be roaring into a helibase for the first time in a year.

Instead of rain, the sun shone down from a sky so crystalline blue that it was hard to credit. High up, he spotted several choppers swooping down toward the camp. A pair of Bell 212 Twin Hueys and a little MD500, all painted the lurid black with red flames of Mount Hood Aviation, just like his car. He'd take that as a good omen.

He let the tail of his classic Firebird Trans Am break loose on the twisting dirt road that climbed through the dense pine woods from the town of Hood

River, perched on the banks of the mighty Columbia and staring up at Mount Hood.

This was gonna be a damn fine summer.

Helibase in the Oregon woods. Nice little town at the foot of the mountain. Hood River was big enough to boast several bars and a pair of breweries. It was also a big windsurfing spot down in the Gorge, which meant the tourists would be young, fit, and primed for some fun. The promise of some serious sport for a footloose and fancy-free guy.

And fire.

He'd missed the bulk of last summer.

He hammered in the clutch and down-shifted to regain control of his fishtail, did his best to ignore the twinge in his new left knee.

Steve had spent last summer on the surgeon's table. And hated every goddamn second he'd been away from the fight. It sure hadn't helped him score much, either. "I used to be a smokejumper until I blew out my knee." Blew up his knee would more accurate since they'd barely saved the leg. Either way, the pickup line just didn't sweep 'em off their feet the way you'd like. Compare that with, "I parachute into forest fires for the fun of it."

Way, way better.

And never again.

He fouled that thought into the bleachers with all the force he could muster and punched the accelerator hard.

Folks would be milling around at the camp if those choppers meant there was an active fire today. As any entrance made was worth making properly, Steve cranked the wheel and jerked up on the emergency brake as he flew into the gravel parking lot.

A dozen heads turned.

He planted a full, four-wheel drift across the lot and fired a broad spray of gravel at a battered old blue-and-rust Jeep as he slid in beside it. Ground to a perfect parallel-parked stop. Bummer that whatever sucker owned the Jeep had taken off the cloth covers and doors. Steve had managed to spray the gravel high enough to land some on the seats.

Excellent.

He settled his wrap-around Porsche Design sunglasses solidly on the bridge of his nose and pulled on his autographed San Francisco Giants cap. The four winning pitchers of the 2012 World Series had signed it. He only wore it when appearances really mattered. Wouldn't do at all to sweat it up.

He hopped out of the car.

Okay, his brain imagined that he hopped out of the car.

His body opened the door, and he managed to swing his left leg out without having to cup a hand behind the knee. Pretty good when you considered he wasn't even supposed to be driving a manual transmission yet. And he'd "accidentally" left his cane at the roadside motel room back in Grants Pass where he'd crashed into bed last night.

So done with that.

Now he stood, that itself the better part of a miracle, on a helibase and felt ready to go.

He debated between tracking down a cup of coffee or finding the base commander to check in. Then he opted for the third choice, the radio shack. The heartbeat of any firebase was its radio tower, and this one actually had a tower. It looked like a very short fire watchtower. Crisscrossed braces and a set of stairs led up to a second-story radio shack with windows and a narrow walkway all around the outside. All of the action would funnel through there for both air and ground crews.

An exterior wooden staircase led in switchbacks up to the shack. The staircase had a broad landing midway that gave him an excuse to stop and survey the scene. And rest his knee.

He could have done worse. Much worse.

Hoodie One helibase was nestled deep in the Cascade Mountains just north of Mount Hood. From here, he could see the icy cap of the eleven-thousand-foot-high dormant volcano towering above everything else in the neighborhood. A long, lenticular cloud shadowed the peak, a jaunty blemish in the otherwise perfect blue sky.

The air smelled both odd and right at the same time. The dry oak and sage smell of his native California had been replaced with wet and pine. You could smell the wet despite the hot summer sun. At least he supposed it was hot. Even in early summer, Oregon was fifteen to twenty degrees cooler than Sacramento in the spring. Sometimes the California air was so parched that it hurt to breathe, but here the air was a balm as he inhaled again.

Ah, there.

He inhaled again deeply.

Every wildfire airbase had it, the sting of aviation fuel and the tang of retardant overridden with a sheen that might be hard work and sweat. It let him know he'd come home.

The firebase had been carved into a high meadow bordered by towering conifers. Only the one dirt road climbing up the hills from the town a half dozen miles below. A line of scrungy metal huts, a rough wooden barracks, and a mess hall that might have been left over from a summer camp for kids a couple decades back. You certainly didn't visit firefighting bases for the luxury of it all.

You came here for the fire. And for what lay between the radio tower on which he perched and the grass-strip runway.

A couple of small fixed-wing Cessnas and a twin-prop Beech Baron were parked along the edge. They'd be used for spotter and lead planes. These planes would fly lead for each run of the big fixed-wing air tankers parked down at the Hood River airport or flying in from other states for the truly big fires.

Then there was the line of helicopters.

The 212s and the MD500 he'd spotted coming in were clearly new arrivals. Crews

were pulling the big, orange Bambi Buckets
from the cargo bays and running out the
lines for the 212s. The MD500 had a built-
in tank. Someone crawled under the belly
of each of the 212s and hooked up the
head of the long lead line used to carry the
bucket two hundred feet below the bird
and the controls to release the valve from
inside the helicopter.

There must be a fire in action. Sure
enough. He could see the refueling truck
headed their way, and it was not moving
at some leisurely pace. Not just action, but
somewhere nearby.

With a start, he realized that he wouldn't
have to go trolling off base for company.
He'd always been careful not to fraternize
with the jump crews, because that made for
a mess when it went south. But if he wasn't
jumping anymore…

Some very fit women would be coming
into this camp as well.

He breathed the air deeply again, trying
to taste just a bit of smoke, and found

it. Damn, but this was gonna be a fine summer.

***

"Climb and left twenty degrees."

As the pilot turned, Carly Thomas leaned until the restraint harness dug into her shoulders so that she could see as much as possible. The front windscreen of the helicopter was sectioned off by instrument panels. She could look over them, under them, or out the side windows of her door, but she still felt like she couldn't see.

She really needed to get her head outside in the air to follow what the fire was doing. Taste it, feel the heat on her face as it climbed the ridge. Could they stop the burn, or would the conflagration jump the craggy barrier and begin its destruction of the next valley?

She needed the air.

But the doors on this thing didn't open in flight, so she couldn't get her face out in the wind. In the little MD500s she could do that; they flew without the doors all the time.

This was her first flight in Mount Hood Aviation's brand-new Firehawk. It might rank as a critical addition to MHA's fire-fighting fleet, but she was far from liking it yet. The fire-rigged Sikorsky Black Hawk felt heavy. The MD500 could carry four people at its limit, and this bird could carry a dozen without noticing. The heavy beat of the rotors was well muffled by the radio headset, but she could feel the pulse against her body.

And she couldn't smell anything except new plastic and paint job.

Available at fine retailers everywhere
More information at: www.mlbuchman.com